The Great Big Book of Monsters, Goblins, Dragons and Giants

John Malam

QED

QED Publishing

First published in the UK in 2009 by
QED Publishing
A Quarto Group Company
226 City Road
London EC1V 2TT

www.qed-publishing.co.uk

ISBN 978 1 84835 333 6

Author John Malam
Editor Amanda Learmonth
Designer Lisa Peacock
Illustrator Vincent Folens

Publisher Steve Evans
Creative Director Zeta Davies
Managing Editor Amanda Askew

Printed and bound in China

Words in **bold** are explained in the glossary on page 116.

Picture credits
(t=top, b=bottom, l=left, r=right, c=centre, fc=front cover)
Alamy Images 11 Mary Evans Picture Library, 16 Mary Evans Picture Library, 19 Les Gibbon, 30t Lars S. Madsen, 35bl Pictures Colour Library, 39 The London Art Archive, 43t INTERFOTO Pressebildagentur, 43b Leslie Garland Picture Library, 47b Mary Evans Picture Library, 51 Pictor International/Image State, 57t Malcolm Park Astronomy images, 63cr The Natural History Museum, 70 North Wind Picture Archives, 95 Michael Runkel Greece, 97 Mary Evans Picture Library, 98b Pictorial Press Ltd, 99 Mary Evans Picture Library, 105t INTERFOTO Pressebildagentur, 107b Redmond Durrell, 108b Tony Watson, 109t Malcolm Park London Events, 111b David Lyons
Bridgeman Art Library 30b Private Collection/Look and Learn, 63br Ashmolean Museum, University of Oxford, UK, 104 British Library, London, UK/British Library Board, 103 Nationalmuseum, Stockholm, Sweden
Corbis 10b Th e Irish Image Collection, 17b Bettmann, 21t Bettmann, 21b Bob Krist, 41b Bettmann, 59 Lindsay Hebberd, 87 Ainaco, 90 Historical Picture Library
Dreamstime 53
Getty Images 7br The Bridgeman Art Library/John Atkinson Grimshaw, 9r Photographer's Choice/Charles Briscoe-Knight, 34t The Image Bank/Chris Alan Wilton, 34b Visuals Unlimited/Ken Lucas, 45t AFP/Stringer, 45c Lonely Planet Image/Jane Sweeney, 77br The Bridgeman Art Library/Boleslas Biegas, 115b Photographer's Choice/Pamela E Reed
Istockphoto 35bc Maris Zemgalietis
Mary Evans Picture Library 7cl Arthur Rackham, 7cc, 7bc Arthur Rackham, 35tr, 35cr, 71t, 91tr, 91tl, 98t, 102t Edwin Wallace
Photolibrary 15b Halfdark, 55 Robert Harding Travel, 73 Thomas Hallstein, 84 Walter Bibikow, 85 Loraine Wilson
Photoshot 93 De Agostini, 102b World Pictures
Scala Archive 79t, 81
Science Photo Library 17t
Shutterstock 7bl Nickolay Marcinkevich, 13b Anthony Hall, 25t Richard Griffin, 35tc Martina Orlich, 35br Javarman, 50 Jean-Michel Olives, 62b Janprchal, 69b Arlen E Breiholz, 75t Canismaior, Temple University/College of Liberal Arts 65t, 109b Timo Kohlbacher, 111t Joe Gough
Topham Picturepoint 6 Charles Walker, 7tl Fortean/Richard Svensson, 7tr Charles Walker, 7cr Fortean/Klaus Aarsleff, 15t, 18b Fortean/Philip Panton, 27t, 28–29, 31 Fortean, 35tl Fortean, 37 The British Library, 62t Charles Walker, 62tl Charles Walker, 63bc Fortean, 67b Alinari, 71b Charles Walker, 75b Charles Walker, 83, 91tc Fortean/Svensson, 91cc Fortean/Svensson, 113t Fortean Picture Library
Werner Foreman 63cc Christie's, London

CONTENTS

Goblins and fairies, dragons, monsters and giants have long been the subjects of folklore and legends all over the world. Prepare to enter their realm of magic, myth and make-believe...

Goblins

and other fairies

CONTENTS

The world of goblins and fairies

For as long as anyone can remember, stories have been told about shy creatures we call fairies, or sometimes **fays.** It's thought that these magical beings live alongside humans in a secret world all of their own. Some fairies live in **clans**, or groups, but many prefer to live alone.

➡ *We generally think of fairies as beautiful, kind beings.*

Be careful what you say

Some believe it is unlucky to say the word 'fairy'. For this reason, it's thought wiser to call them 'little folk', 'good neighbours', or 'hidden people'.

All fairies look like humans, but they have powers that no human can ever hope to master. These timid creatures are rarely seen, but when they come into the world of people, strange things happen. Some fairy folk such as goblins love to play tricks and make nuisances of themselves. Other fairies such as brownies are good and help the humans they meet.

Who's who in fairyland?

Brownies

These are helpful fairies that often live in human homes where they do useful work.

Gnomes

These fairies live in the earth where they guard great treasures.

Goblins

These are bad-tempered, ugly fairies that live in dark places and make trouble for humans.

Hobgoblins

Although similar to goblins, hobgoblins are not as mischievous.

Dwarfs

These hard-working fairies live underground and help humans when it suits them.

Elves

Light elves are friendly, kind fairies, but dark elves play tricks on humans.

Nymphs

These fairies live among rivers, seas, trees, meadows and mountains.

Pixies

Similar to elves, pixies do good and bad things to humans.

Once upon a time:
How the Nereids saved Jason

This myth comes from...

In a land far away, a ram's fleece hung from a tree. It was a skin like no other, for it shimmered with gold.

There came a time when Jason, a prince of Greece, set out to take the Golden Fleece. It seemed an impossible task, as he faced many dangers, but the gods were on his side. The golden treasure soon fell into Jason's hands.

The Clashing Rocks

The Clashing Rocks were found in the Bosporus Strait, a narrow passage of water with high rocks on either side. It joins the Black Sea to the Sea of Marmara, in modern-day Turkey.

➡ *The Bosporus Strait is a narrow passage of water where the Clashing Rocks were said to be found.*

On the voyage home to Greece, Jason had to sail between the Clashing Rocks. Many a ship had been crushed by these deadly rocks, but Jason's good fortune continued. The Nereids, who were the fairies or nymphs of the sea, rose up from beneath the waters and lifted his ship to safety. After this, the nymphs returned to their secret home under the sea, ready to guide other sailors to safety.

NEREIDS

The **Nereids** were the daughters of the sea god Nereus. There were 50 Nereids, all of whom were young and beautiful. They rode through the sea on creatures called **hippocamps**, which were part-horse part-fish.

➡ *The Nereids lifted Jason's ship onto the crests of the waves, safely beyond the reach of the deadly Clashing Rocks.*

Fairies that live in troops

Fairies are similar to humans in many ways. Just like people, some fairies live together in communities or clans.

These are called **trooping fairies** and they like nothing better than to troop or parade in colourful processions, with lots of dancing, feasting, singing and music. They are ruled over by kings and queens, and each year they celebrate the great festivals of **Beltane** and **Samhain**.

➡ *At the festival of Samhain, fairies sing and dance, watched over by the king and queen.*

⬇ *All that's left of this burial mound in Ireland is the stone chamber inside it, where a person was once buried. Today, it's said to be the home of the Little Folk.*

The most famous trooping fairies live in Ireland, British Isles. They are the Daoine Sídhe (say: *deena shee*) or Little Folk, who live in and around the country's ancient **burial mounds** and lonely thorn trees. Daoine Sídhe fairies are tall and thin, with beautiful faces, sweet voices and long, flowing hair.

The blood that flows through their veins is pure white. They try to remain out of sight of humans, but if disturbed they make bad things happen. Humans suddenly fall ill and farmers' crops mysteriously die. Worst of all, babies are stolen and fairy babies called **changelings** are left in their place.

However, the Little Folk do have a good side. Humans who are unwell leave them gifts of food, hoping the fairies will use their magic to heal them.

fairy festivals

In the world of fairies, there are two seasons – summer and winter. The festival of Beltane (1 May) marks the start of summer, and the festival of Samhain (31 October) is the start of winter.

Changelings

A changeling is a fairy baby swapped for a human baby. This can only happen if the human baby has not been **baptized** (given its name in a religious ceremony). If the human parents discover it is a fairy baby, the changeling will vanish and the human child will be sent home alive and well.

If a human family is left with a changeling child, the infant cries constantly and grows up into a weakling.

Once upon a time:
The girl who dances with a fairy king

Fairy protector

In Ireland, British Isles, Finvarra is known as the protecting spirit of the family. This is because he once returned a kidnapped woman, Etain, safely to her home. If humans are kind to him, he rewards them with good harvests and fine horses.

There was once a young girl who was loved by Finvarra, king of the Irish fairies. Every night the fairies came to her house and led her away to dance with the king.

The more she danced, the more she wanted to live with the Little Folk forever. Then, as night became day, they vanished, and she awoke in her bed.

One day, she told her friends what happened to her at night. They said she must have been dreaming, but the girl said it was all true. To prove it, she would show the fairies to them.

➡ *The young girl danced and danced with King Finvarra.*

That night, she took her friends to where the fairies met, but as it was dark and cold they grew frightened and ran back to their homes. The girl was left to wait on her own. The fairies came, and as she danced the night away she wished to be with them forever.

The fairies granted her wish and her spirit passed from the human world into the fairy world. From then on, she lived among the Little Folk. If you know where to look, you might see her dancing with King Finvarra.

Finvarra, the kind-hearted king of the Irish fairies.

This hill at Knockmaa, County Galway, Ireland, is said to be King Finvarra's home.

Fairies that live alone

Some fairies spend their entire lives on their own. They are called **solitary fairies**. They want to be left alone either because they are terribly shy, or because they find it hard to get along with other fairies.

Whatever the reason for living alone, these fairies are always connected with particular places, such as the homes of humans, woodlands or ancient burial mounds.

Solitary fairies can be complete opposites. Some, such as brownies, are helpful and kind towards humans. Others, such as goblins, can be mischievous. A human family should hope that a brownie comes to live with them in their home, not a goblin. For a small reward, such as a bowl of fresh milk left out at night, a brownie will work while humans sleep.

← A goblin in the house means one thing – trouble!

In the morning, the humans will wake to find the house magically cleaned from top to bottom. However, if a goblin moves in, the household chores will be left undone. Instead, this unwelcome guest will spread dust, break plates, hide things and make a mess.

⬆ *Morgan le Fay was a magician as well as a fairy. Here, she brews a potion while she says a magic spell.*

Changing their shape

Some solitary fairies are **shape-shifters** – they can change into creatures of beauty, hideous beings or even become invisible. Morgan le Fay (the Fairy) is a shape-shifter who can change into a bird and fly away.

⬆ *Spilled milk is a gift for the fairies.*

Spilled milk

Milk is a favourite drink of all fairies. If any is spilled by a human, it should be left where it falls as a gift for the fairies. It should never be cleaned up because the fairies will think their present is being taken from them.

Once upon a time:
The fairy who changed shape

This myth comes from...

One moonless night, a group of men were crossing a dark, lonely heath, somewhere in England.

A mischievous hobgoblin lived on the heath, and he watched as the men tried to find their way home. The **sprite** was Robin Goodfellow who, though he was good by name, was not always good by deed. He played tricks on people, as the travellers were about to discover.

Robin Goodfellow loved to play tricks on lost travellers.

Robin Goodfellow went up to the men and offered to show them the way. Thinking they had found a true friend, the men set off after him. As they followed their guide, Robin Goodfellow shifted his shape. The hobgoblin changed into a **will-o'-the-wisp** – a strange, flickering light that made him look like a walking fire.

Night light

At night, balls of light can sometimes be seen glowing low over swamps and marshes. They are known as will-o'-the-wisps. They are probably caused by natural gas from rotting plants catching fire.

Will-o'-the-wisps are also known as foolish fire, as travellers often mistake them for lights in houses.

Wherever he went, the men went, too. Up the heath and down it, all night long. Only when the first rays of sunlight appeared was the spell lifted. Robin Goodfellow sent the weary men on their way with the sound of his laughter ringing in their ears.

Shakespeare's fairy play

In William Shakespeare's play 'A Midsummer Night's Dream', Robin Goodfellow plays the part of a fairy called Puck. There are other fairies in the play, including Oberon and Titania, the king and queen of the fairies.

This painting shows Puck, who faces us, near the middle, from Shakespeare's 'A Midsummer Night's Dream'.

Mischievous elves

A race of magical creatures lives in the colder countries of northern Europe. In Denmark they are called 'ellen', in Germany 'alfar', in Sweden 'elvor' and in Britain they are called elves.

These fairies all look like miniature humans – elf men are always ugly, elf women always beautiful. They make their homes in dark forests, often in hollowed-out tree trunks or ancient burial mounds.

Elves live deep in the forest in secret, hideaway places.

*A prehistoric flint arrowhead, or '**elf arrow**'.*

Elf arrows

Thousands of years ago, human hunters used arrows with points made from pieces of flint. In parts of Europe, some people used to call them elf arrows.

BLAME IT ON ELVES

Elves get the blame for many things.

- If you have knots and tangles in your hair, you have elf locks.
- Plants and trees twisted out of shape are known as elf twisted.
- A strange fire at night over a swamp or marsh is an elf fire.
- If a person suffers a mysterious illness they have an elf shot.
- Another word for a birthmark is an elf mark.

The elf race can be divided into elves that live above ground (light elves) and those that live underground (dark elves). Light elves are friendly, but dark elves are not.

A twisted, knotted tree is thought to be the work of elves.

Dark elves cast spells over humans that last for years. They steal milk and bread, and will swap their own babies for human children. A human family tricked into bringing up an elf child will suffer years of misery.

Once upon a time:
Rip Van Winkle and the elves

Rip Van Winkle was a man who lived in a village at the foot of the Catskill Mountains. One day, he went hunting in the woods near his home.

As evening drew near, Rip began his journey home. On the way, he met a small man with a long beard and bushy hair. He was dressed in old-fashioned clothes and was carrying a heavy barrel of wine. He was an elf.

The elf asked for help, so Rip took his barrel and followed him to a clearing where there were other elves, all playing ninepins. The elves drank the wine – and so did Rip. Before long, he fell fast asleep.

➡ *The mischievous elves caused Rip Van Winkle to sleep for 20 years.*

When Rip woke up, the sun was in the sky. Thinking he had slept the night on the mountain, he hurried home, but his village seemed different. A crowd gathered to look at the stranger, and when Rip told them his name, he was met by puzzled looks. Rip Van Winkle, they said, had left the village 20 years ago, and had never been seen from that day to this.

← The story of Rip Van Winkle was written in 1819 by American author Washington Irving.

→ Ninepins is an older version of skittles and bowling.

The game of ninepins

Ninepins is similar to the modern games of bowling and skittles. Nine bottle-shaped pins are arranged in the shape of a diamond. Wooden balls are rolled to knock the pins down.

Gruesome goblins

If it's knee-high to a human, always grumpy and has an ugly, wrinkled face, it's probably a goblin. These unpleasant creatures spell trouble for humans. Some live as **house fairies** and make nuisances of themselves.

Goblins only come out at night, when they love to cause mischief..

Hello to a hobgoblin

If you had to choose between a hobgoblin and a goblin in the house, pick a hobgoblin. It's just as ugly as a goblin, but hairier, and will be helpful rather than harmful.

Goodbye to a goblin

The only way to rid a home of a goblin is to scatter flax seeds on the floor. He won't have time to pick up all the tiny seeds before dawn, which will really annoy him! If you do the same over the next few nights, the goblin will get so fed up, he'll leave the house.

House goblins enjoy making floorboards creak, rattling handles, knocking on doors and snatching blankets off sleeping people. It's no wonder that humans often think their house is haunted by a ghost.

Not all goblins spend their lives in the homes of humans. Some are found in human workplaces, especially underground places such as mines. Others lurk under rocks or among the twisted roots of ancient trees.

➡ *Scattering flax seeds on the floor is a good way to get rid of a goblin.*

Once upon a time:
The goblins who live underground

Deep inside the mountains of Bohemia, in central Europe, lies a great treasure. Locked within the ancient rocks is a precious store of silver ore, the raw material of silver coins and jewellery. For hundreds of years, miners have dug into the mountains, as if they were rabbits burrowing into hills.

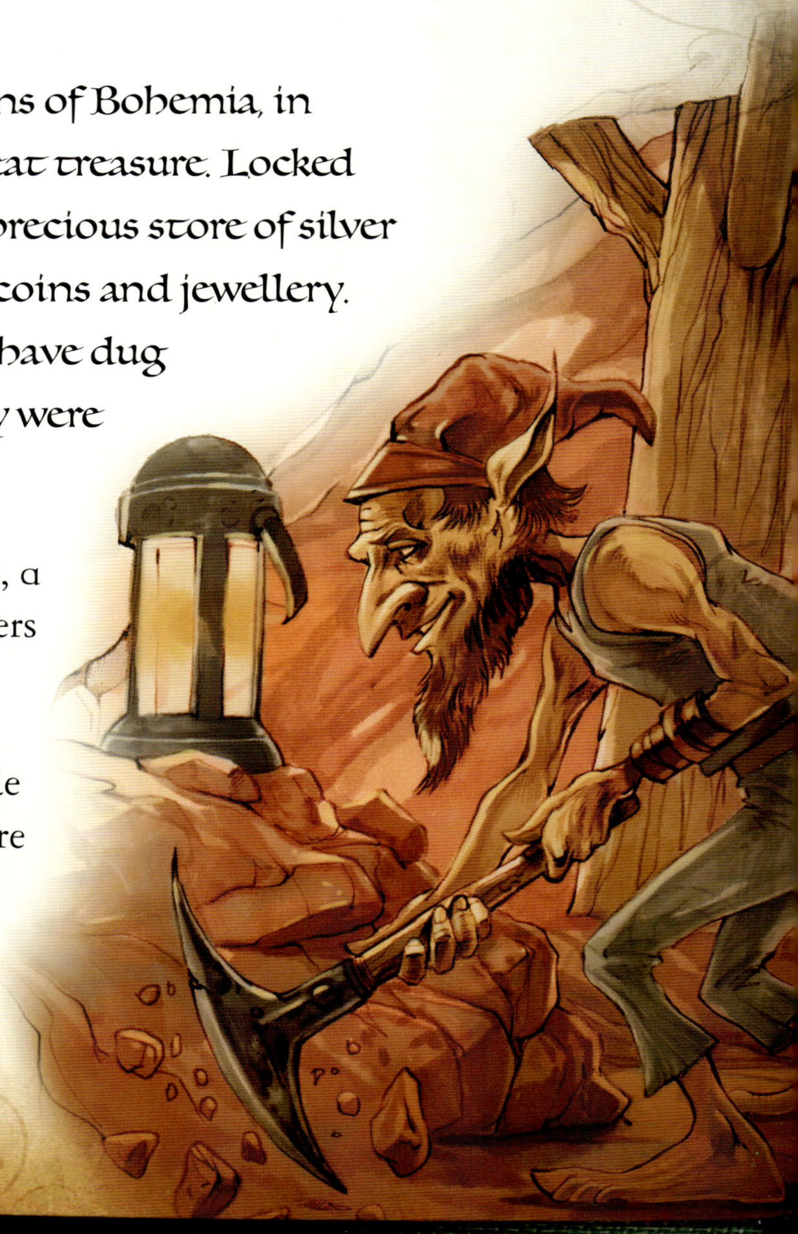

At the silver mines of Kutná Hora, a town in the Czech Republic, workers tell tales of mine spirits they call Wichtlein (Little Wights). These underground goblins look like little old men with long beards. They are dressed as miners and they carry lanterns, mallets and hammers.

KNOCK, KNOCK

The tin mines of Cornwall, England, are also said to be home to noisy goblins. They are known as Knockers, as the sound of knocking could often be heard from deep within the mine.

⬆ *Tin mines like this one in Cornwall are believed to be home to goblins called Knockers.*

As the miners work, small stones rain down on them. This, so they say, is the work of the goblins. The goblins also guide the miners to the silver. They knock from inside the rock to tell the miners if they are close to the ore. However, the knocking can also signal danger – three loud knocks warns a miner that he is about to die.

⬅ *The goblins of Kutná Hora use axes to knock from inside the rock, guiding miners to the silver.*

Gifts for goblins

The Wichtlein goblins expect to be brought gifts of food every day. If not, they will take their revenge by showering the miners with more stones.

Dreadful dwarfs

At first sight, it's quite easy to confuse a dwarf with a goblin, as both races are short, grey and wrinkly.

If you look at their legs and feet, the differences become clear. While goblins have straight legs and feet, dwarfs' legs are curved, and their feet can even point backwards. For this reason, dwarfs always wear boots.

Toads and toad-stones

People have long believed that toads are dwarfs in disguise. It was thought each toad carried a jewel, and if a person wore this '**toad-stone**' as a lucky charm, they would be protected from harm.

A dwarf works underground to make precious objects, such as crowns.

The Seven Dwarfs

'Snow White and the Seven Dwarfs' is a famous film made by Walt Disney in 1937. It was based on a German fairy tale, in which a girl called Snowdrop met seven helpful dwarfs. In the film, Snowdrop became Snow White, and the dwarfs were given funny names such as Grumpy and Sneezy.

➡ *In the film 'Snow White and the Seven Dwarfs', the dwarfs were called Bashful, Doc, Dopey, Grumpy, Happy, Sleepy and Sneezy.*

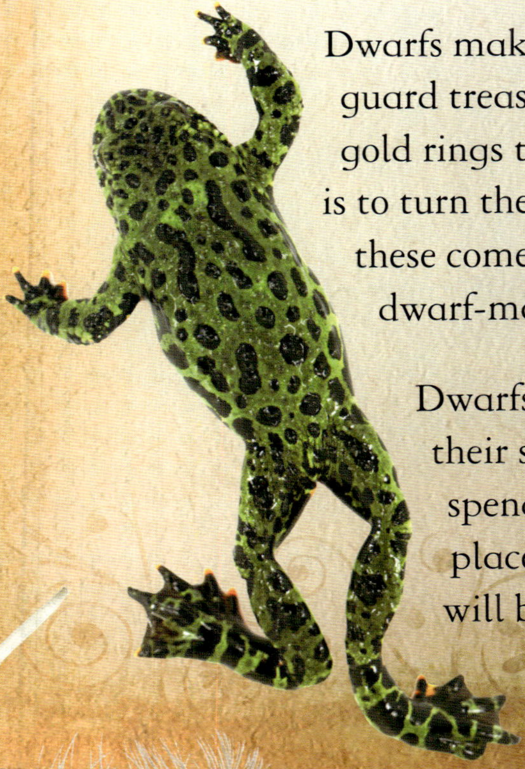

Dwarfs make their homes underground. They guard treasures of jewels and precious metals, from gold rings to swords fit for a hero. Their special gift is to turn these riches into beautiful objects. However, these come at a price for the new owner – if it's dwarf-made, it will probably carry a curse.

Dwarfs are rarely seen by humans. They can change their shape as they wish, and it is said that they spend the daytime as toads lurking in damp, dark places. If they are touched by the sun's light, they will be turned instantly to stone.

Once upon a time:
Rumplestiltskin

Once there was a man who boasted to a king that his daughter could spin straw into gold. It wasn't true, but the king believed the man and ordered the girl to make him some gold.

Left alone at her spinning wheel, the girl began to cry. Her sobbing reached the ears of a dwarf, and that night he called on her. The dwarf promised to spin the straw into gold, in return for the girl's necklace. The king was delighted with the gold, but he was greedy and wanted more.

That night, the dwarf returned and spun more gold, and in return the girl paid him with her ring. Again, the king demanded more, and the dwarf came and did his magic a third time. As the girl had nothing left to give the dwarf, a bargain was struck. She agreed to give the dwarf her first child.

The importance of names

Names are important in stories about fairies. If a human baby is not baptized, it is un-named. This means it is at risk of being snatched by fairies. Also, calling out the name of a fairy is believed to be a way of making it appear.

Rumpelstiltskin was a dwarf who could spin straw into gold.

The girl married the king, and after a year she had a child. One night, the dwarf came to take the baby, but the girl refused.

The dwarf said that she could keep the infant only if she could discover the dwarf's name. Messengers travelled the land to find out. In one place, they overheard a curious little man gleefully calling out his name and saying he was soon to take a human child.

The dwarf returned, and when the girl said his name was Rumpelstiltskin, the evil creature cried out in rage and stamped so hard that he tore himself in two and died.

Fairy magic

If there's one thing above all that fairies are famous for, it's magic.

When a **milk tooth** falls out, you probably put it under your pillow at bedtime and hope for a visit from the **tooth fairy**. A **fairy godmother** might make good things happen to you – but only as long as you believe in the magic of fairyland.

⬆ *Fairies are said to meet inside toadstool rings.*

Circles of ancient stones or rings of toadstools are said to be magical places where fairies meet. A human that joins fairies inside a fairy ring crosses over from this world into a mysterious place where strange things happen.

FAMOUS FAIRY GODMOTHER

In the much-loved fairy tale of Cinderella, a servant girl's life is changed forever thanks to her fairy godmother. The young girl changes into a rich woman, and she is freed from her hard-working life.

➡ *The Fairy Godmother used her magic to help Cinderella go to the prince's ball.*

Fairy magic makes the human invisible to other humans, and they lose all sense of time. A few hours spent dancing in a fairy ring may turn out to be many human years.

Fairies cast their magic over humans in many ways. Even though they don't exist in real life, they will always live inside our imaginations. Fairy stories have been told for hundreds of years, and will continue to be told for many more.

fairy fakers

In 1917, two girls made paper cut-outs of fairies and took pictures of them in their garden. Elsie Wright and Frances Griffiths, from Bradford, England, told people they had seen real fairies, and many people believed them.

A photo of Frances Griffiths with her paper fairies, taken by Elsie Wright. After more than 60 years, the girls (who were then old ladies) finally admitted that their fairies weren't real.

Dragons

CONTENTS

The world of dragons

Stories have been told about dragons for thousands of years. Countries all over the world have myths about these fabulous creatures, and there are many tales that speak of the daring deeds of **dragon-slayers**.

Dragons are often described as the guardians of valuable treasure or captured princesses. They are among the most dangerous of all mythical creatures, and the hardest to defeat. All dragons have scaly skin. Many have fiery breath or poisonous, stinging tails. Some have wings, others don't. Some are short, others are long and have the twisting bodies of giant **serpents**.

The dragon is one of the most fabulous creatures in mythology.

Dinosaur skeletons may have led people to believe in dragons.

From dinosaur to dragon

Long ago, when ancient bones from dinosaurs were found in the ground, no one knew what creatures they had come from. These mysterious bones might have led people to make up stories about terrifying creatures, such as dragons.

Who's who among the dragons?

Dragons from European folklore

Cockatrice

A monster with a dragon's body and wings, and the head and legs of a cockerel.

European dragon

A fire-breathing, winged beast with scaly skin, long legs and sharp claws.

Worm

A dragon with a huge, snake-like body.

Basilisk

Similar to the cockatrice, but with eight cockerel legs and a poisonous bite.

Dragons from folklore around the world

Chinese and Japanese dragon

A lizardlike beast without wings but with a horned head, scaly skin and sharp claws.

Babylonian and ancient Middle Eastern dragon

A wingless beast with eagle's legs at the rear and cat's legs at the front.

Indian dragon

A monstrous serpent with three heads.

Dragons of Europe

Ever since the time of the ancient Greeks, 2500 years ago, dragons have been part of European mythology.

The ancient Greeks thought of dragons as massive serpents that lived at the ends of the world where they guarded great treasures. The most famous was Ladon, a giant serpent with 100 heads and 200 fiery eyes. It guarded a tree of golden apples.

European dragons are often described as winged beasts with fiery breath.

Saints and dragons

In Christian mythology, St. George is a well-known dragon-slayer. He was not the only **saint** to defeat a dragon. St. Martha managed to tame Tarasque, a dragon that terrified the south of France.

During Roman times (about 2000 years ago), the Romans spoke of dragons that lived in Ethiopia, East Africa. It was believed these monsters were snakelike creatures that breathed fire, had wings, were about 18 metres long and ate the flesh of elephants.

➡ *This page from a 'bestiary' (a book about beasts from the Middle Ages) shows what dragons were thought to look like.*

Dragons at war

When Roman soldiers went into battle in the AD 300s, a dragon went with them. It was a **standard** (a type of flag), shaped as a dragon-headed serpent. In the AD 600s, a red dragon became a symbol of Wales, UK. Warriors carried dragon flags into battle. The greatest warriors were given the title **'pendragon'**, meaning 'dragon head', or leader.

At the start of the **Middle Ages** (from about AD 450), dragons were seen as evil creatures. Myths spoke of Christian saints whose duty was to slay dragons and defeat evil. Between the 1100s and 1400s, books known as 'bestiaries' described dragons in great detail. People believed these monsters really existed.

Once upon a time:
Beowulf and the dragon

In the kingdom of the Danes, the monster Grendel struck fear into the hearts of all men. Each night, Grendel came from the swamp, and no matter how hard they fought, the Danes were always defeated.

➡ *Beowulf was a dragon-slayer and hero of the Danes.*

In time, a warrior called Beowulf came to Denmark and killed Grendel. When the monster's mother wanted revenge, he killed her, too. Beowulf became a hero, and his fame spread far and wide.

Many years later, Beowulf fought a dragon that guarded buried treasure. Thieves disturbed the dragon in its **lair**, and it breathed fire across the land.

➡ *A gold clasp from the Sutton Hoo treasure. It is decorated with red stones called garnets.*

The Sutton Hoo treasure

In 1939, gold and silver treasure was found inside a **burial mound** at Sutton Hoo, Suffolk, England. It is believed to have belonged to a king from the AD 600s. Like Beowulf, the king was buried inside an earthen mound. This was the custom at the time for some important people.

Beowulf took up his sword. He fought the dragon, but its scales were like armour and Beowulf's weapon was useless.

Another warrior came to Beowulf's help, and between them the dragon was killed. But there was a price to pay. Beowulf had been bitten by the dragon. As its deadly poison flowed through his veins, his life came to an end. The warrior was laid to rest with great treasure in a burial mound beside the sea.

Once upon a time:
The man who became a dragon

This myth comes from…

Greed is a terrible thing and there are those who never learn this. Take a man called Fafnir, and his brothers Ottar and Regin.

Ottar was able to change himself into other beings. One day, he changed into an otter. The god Loki thought he was a real otter, and killed him. The brothers' father then demanded Loki pay for his crime. Loki did this, by giving him gold, but the gold was **cursed**, so bad luck would always follow it.

The greedy brothers killed their father and stole his gold.

When they saw their father's gold, Fafnir and Regin were filled with greed. The brothers killed their father, but Fafnir stole the gold and ran far away. He changed into a terrifying dragon, and lay on the treasure to guard it.

Regin wanted revenge, and he wanted the treasure. He went to Sigurd, a brave warrior, for help. Regin gave him a magic sword, which Sigurd used to slay Fafnir the dragon. Regin claimed the treasure, but the curse passed on to him. Regin was killed by Sigurd, who took the treasure for himself. Then the curse was again passed on, and he, too, was doomed to die.

➡ *Sigurd slayed Fafnir the dragon with his magic sword.*

⬅ *A Viking 'drakkar', or **dragonship**.*

Sigurd the dragon-slayer

After Sigurd killed Fafnir, he licked the blood from his fingers. This gave him the power to understand the language of birds. Two birds then told him that Regin planned to kill him.

Dragonships

The story of Fafnir the dragon was told by the **Vikings** of Scandinavia and northern Europe. Some of their **longships** had carvings of dragons' heads on their prows (fronts). The Vikings called these ships 'drakkar', or dragon ships.

Once upon a time:
The dragon that crash-landed

In the year 1421, a dragon was flying to Mount Pilatus, near Lucerne, Switzerland. It was one of the many dragons that lived in caves high on the mountain's snowy peak.

On its way home, the dragon crashed to the ground and startled a farmer who was out walking. When the farmer, whose name was Stempflin, saw the great beast flapping its wings and trying to take off, he fainted.

Stempflin had no idea how long he lay on the ground, but he awoke with a start. He looked for the dragon, but it was nowhere to be seen. Would anyone believe his story, or would they say he had fallen asleep and had a dream?

Helpful dragons

Unlike many dragons, the Mount Pilatus dragons are thought of as friendly and helpful. They are believed to heal the sick and rescue travellers lost in the mountains.

⬇ *The dragon crashed to the ground, startling Farmer Stempflin.*

⬆ *Mount Pilatus is believed to be the home of the friendly dragons.*

⬆ *Cinnabar is a red-coloured stone, also known as a 'dragon-stone'.*

WHAT IS A DRAGON-STONE?

Red-coloured stones are sometimes called '**dragon-stones**'. They are thought to be hardened lumps of dragons' blood.

The confused farmer went over to where the dragon had crashed, and saw a pool of blood. It was the dragon's blood, and in the middle was a strange, red stone. Stempflin knew it to be a dragon-stone. He picked it up and took it home. From that day on it brought him good luck, as it had the power to cure any illness or injury.

Dragons of the Middle East

Some of the world's first dragon stories ever told come from the countries of the Middle East. These tales were told by ancient peoples known as Sumerians, Babylonians and Assyrians.

The stories go back about 5000 years. They describe how the world began, and the struggle between the forces of good and evil. Dragons were thought of as evil monsters that people had to kill or make peace with.

Dragons in the Bible

Dragons are mentioned in the Christian Bible. They may come from stories that spread across the Middle East. For example, in the Bible there is a 'red dragon with seven heads and ten horns'. It stands for the Devil.

Dahak was a serpent monster with two snake heads and one human head.

Anzu was a birdlike monster with a lion's head. It caused sandstorms when it flapped its wings.

⬆ *A dragon picture on the Ishtar Gate, Babylon.*

They came in many forms. Some were imagined as giant serpents, others as creatures made from the body parts of different animals. No matter what they looked like, all of them were powerful and terrifying beings.

Gatekeeper dragons

In ancient times, visitors to the city of Babylon, in modern-day Iraq, walked through a gateway in the city wall. The gateway, which was made about 575 BC, was decorated with pictures of dragons and other fierce creatures. Visitors could have no doubt that they were entering an important, powerful city.

⬇ *Musrussu was a giant serpent with the front feet of a cat, the back legs of a bird and a tail with a poisonous sting.*

⬇ *Tiamat was a huge sea snake with two forelegs, a giant tail and horns on its head.*

⬇ *Leviathan was a sea monster with seven heads and hundreds of eyes.*

Once upon a time:
How the world began

This myth comes from…

In the time before Heaven and Earth were created, only chaos existed. It was a time of nothingness, a time of confusion.

Then, from the nothingness, two creatures appeared. They were Tiamat, the mother of the salty sea, and Abzu, the father of freshwater rivers and lakes. From these beings the first gods were born. One of them was Enki.

As the gods grew, they quarreled. This upset their father Abzu who wished to kill them all. But Enki was cunning – he killed his father to save his own life.

← *The young gods argued and fought each other, which upset their father, Abzu.*

Tiamat, wife of Abzu and mother of Enki, wanted revenge. She became a dragon and led an army of other monsters to destroy Enki and the gods. Only one god was brave enough to fight against Tiamat. He was Marduk, who shot an arrow into Tiamat's mouth that went straight to her heart.

Marduk cut Tiamat's body in two. He used one half to make the heavens and all its stars, and the other half to form the Earth. Her chest became the mountains, and from her eyes flowed the rivers Tigris and Euphrates. This is how the world began.

Marduk aimed his arrow into the dragon Tiamat's mouth.

MARDUK THE DRAGON-SLAYER

Marduk was the chief god of Babylon. Many myths were told about him. He was described as a hero who always defeated the forces of evil.

Marduk (left, in a chariot) fights Tiamat.

Once upon a time:
George and the dragon

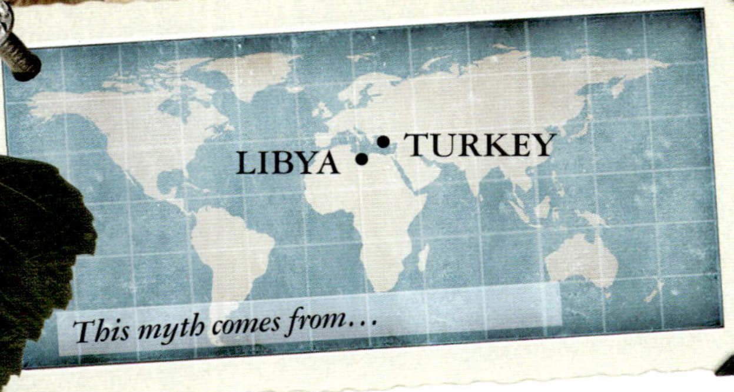

The city of Silene, in Libya, North Africa, was troubled by a dragon. At night, it breathed poison upon the people, who lived in fear of the monster.

Every day, the people took the dragon two sheep, and hoped it would leave them in peace. But there came a time when the townsfolk had used up nearly all their sheep, so they started to leave the dragon one sheep and one human.

The human victim was chosen at random, and one day the king's daughter was picked. At first, the king refused to let his daughter die, but he had no choice. Dressed in her wedding clothes, the princess was taken to the dragon's lair.

The princess shook with fear at the sight of the mighty dragon.

⬆ *George wounded the dragon with his spear, saving the princess's life.*

Life of St. George

St. George came from Cappadocia (part of modern-day Turkey) and lived in the AD 200s. He was a Christian, and he disagreed with the terrible way the Romans were treating the Christians. He was sent to prison by the Romans and killed for refusing to give up his Christian faith.

As the princess awaited her death, a traveller rode by. His name was George. The princess told him about the dragon, and he promised to save her. When the dragon came near, George rode towards it and wounded it with his spear. He told the princess to tie her belt around the dragon's neck and lead it into the city.

Saint day

On 23 April, people celebrate St. George's day. St. George is the **patron saint** of Aragon and Catalonia in Spain, as well as England, Georgia, Lithuania, Palestine, Portugal, Germany and Greece.

On seeing the dragon, people fled in terror. George promised to kill the dragon on one condition – that the king and all his people became Christians. This they did, and so George slayed the monster and saved the townsfolk.

Dragons of China and Japan

The myths of China and Japan tell many stories about dragons. The dragons of China are usually described as friendly towards humans, but Japanese dragons can cause harm.

Both Chinese and Japanese dragons are wingless beasts with snaking, scaly bodies, four short legs and sharp claws. Their heads are small and delicate, with whiskers and wispy beards. They have big ears, horns on their heads and they breathe fire and smoke from their nostrils.

A white dragon and a blue dragon from the myths of China.

Dragons are popular beasts in the folktales of China and Japan.

Dragon colors

Chinese dragons are very colourful. The colours have special meanings.

- A black dragon is in charge of lakes.
- A red dragon is in charge of rivers.
- A blue dragon is kind and brave.
- A yellow dragon can talk to the gods.
- A white dragon means a disaster will happen, such as a **famine**.

In a Chinese dragon dance, a team of dancers carries a colourful dragon made from cloth on poles above their heads.

Dragon dance

The dragon dance is performed in China, at the start of the Chinese New Year. The dance began as a way to please the Chinese gods, in the hope they would give farmers a good year. Today, it is said to bring good luck.

The dragons' eyes are red, and inside their mouths they keep the 'pearl of wisdom' (in China the pearl is a symbol of wisdom). They love jewellery, especially **jade**, and they avoid anything made from **iron** as this can hurt them.

Once upon a time:
The dragon and the phoenix

A dragon and a **phoenix** (a mythical bird) lived on an island. One day, they found a beautiful pebble in the riverbed. They decided to polish the pebble until it became a round, white pearl.

When they were finished, they had created the most perfect treasure. The pearl gave off a soft, glowing light. As time passed, news of the precious pearl spread, until Xi Wangmu (say: *shee wang-moo*), the Queen Mother, learned about it. From this moment, she wanted it.

One night, as the dragon and the phoenix slept, the Queen Mother sent a servant to steal the jewel, and when he returned with the prize, she locked it away.

CHINESE DRAGON NAMES

In China, dragons are called 'lung'. This word is always part of their name. For example, Chang Lung, Ti Lung and Ying Lung are all different kinds of Chinese dragon.

↑ *The dragon became Jade Dragon Mountain.*

The dragon and the phoenix searched their island, but the pearl was nowhere to be found. It was only when they went to the Queen Mother's palace that they saw a familiar light – the light of the pearl.

← *The dragon and the phoenix discover who has taken their precious pearl.*

Inside the palace, the Queen Mother was showing the pearl to her friends. Suddenly, the dragon and the phoenix rushed in to take back their treasure. In the struggle that followed, the pearl was thrown from a window. It hit the ground and became a lake. The dragon and the phoenix settled beside the lake. They became the mountains that still guard the treasure inside the lake from that day to this.

Once upon a time:

How the jellyfish lost its bones

It is said that jellyfish used to have bones, fins and feet. One day it lost them, and this is how it happened.

There was a Dragon King called Ryujin who lived in a wonderful palace at the bottom of the sea, built of red and white **coral**. Ryujin was a powerful dragon and it was he, and he alone, that controlled the tides. Turtles, fish and jellyfish were all his servants.

One day, he ordered Jellyfish to bring Monkey to him, as Ryujin wanted to eat its liver. Jellyfish obeyed his master. When Jellyfish found Monkey, he explained that the Dragon King had asked to see him.

The pair began to swim to Ryujin's underwater palace. On the way, Jellyfish told Monkey what Ryujin planned to do. Monkey thought for a moment, then told Jellyfish that he had left his liver in a jar in the forest. He would gladly go back and collect it, and bring it to the Dragon King later. Jellyfish agreed, so he let Monkey go.

When Jellyfish told Ryujin that Monkey would be late coming to the palace, the Dragon King became angry. He could see that Monkey had tricked Jellyfish. In his rage, Ryujin hit Jellyfish so hard, its bones were crushed out of him – leaving a blob of boneless jelly.

Dragon Kings

Among the dragons of China and Japan are four described as Dragon Kings. These are the most powerful of all dragons, and each of them controls a different sea. In Japan, they are the Dragon King of the East Sea, South Sea, West Sea and North Sea.

*Itsukushima **shrine**, Japan, where the daughter of Dragon King Ryujin is believed to live.*

Dragon shrines

There are shrines (sacred places) in Japan linked with dragons. For example, Itsukushima shrine, on the island of Miyajima, is said to be where the daughter of Dragon King Ryujin lived.

Dragons of India

The ancient stories of India describe dragons and dragonlike creatures that existed at the very beginning of the world. Myths tell of great battles in which dragons are defeated.

As with Chinese and Japanese dragons, those of India are usually pictured as giant, wingless serpents. They have short legs, and some have many heads. Their long bodies are covered in scales. They breathe fire and smoke from their mouths and nostrils.

Vritra, a three-headed dragon.

Dragon hell

The dragons of India are said to live in an underground place known as Patala, which is a form of hell. It is where the souls of wicked humans are sent. They are guarded by dragons, and can never escape.

Ananta, a serpent-dragon with many heads.

MOON-EATING DRAGON

According to an Indian myth, Rahu's dragon head was sliced off and thrown to the heavens, but it could not die. In revenge for being cut off, the head chases the Moon and eats it once a month. Sometimes it bites a chunk out of the Sun, which is when a **solar eclipse** happens – the Moon passes between the Sun and the Earth and blocks out the Sun's light.

Apalala, a serpent-dragon with two legs.

When a solar eclipse took place, people believed the dragon Rahu had bitten a chunk out of the Sun.

The most famous Indian serpent-dragon is Vritra, meaning 'Encloser'. A dragon with three heads, its vast body wrapped itself around the whole world. Another Indian dragon is Rahu, who has the body of a human and the head and tail of a dragon.

Rahu, a human-like monster with a dragon's head and tail.

Once upon a time: The dragon and the sea

This myth comes from...

A priest called Tvashtri wanted his son Trisiras to become king of the gods. The true king was Indra, so when Indra saw that Trisiras was after his throne, he struck him dead.

Tvashtri was beside himself with grief over the death of his son, and he swore revenge against Indra. He created a huge serpent-dragon named Vritra. The serpent was so big it could reach into the heavens, and when Indra wasn't looking, Vritra stretched up and swallowed him.

Indra crawled out of Vritra's stomach and tickled its throat. The dragon spat him out. Indra now tried to fight Vritra, but the monster was always stronger.

➡ *Indra used foam made by the sea to slay the dragon Vritra.*

Indra asked the god Vishnu for advice. Vishnu told him to make peace with Vritra. The dragon agreed, but on condition that Indra never attacked it with any weapon made of wood, metal or stone, with anything dry or wet, or during the day or night.

One day, Indra was by the sea. The sun was going down, so it was neither day nor night. A huge wave washed onto the shore, sending up a column of foam. Indra realized the foam wasn't wood, stone or metal, and wasn't wet or dry. He seized the foam and brought it crashing down on Vritra, and the dragon was killed.

The rains come

In some versions of the Vritra myth, the serpent is said to have drunk all Earth's water, causing a terrible drought. But when Indra killed it, he released the trapped water from the serpent's body, causing the rain to fall.

This temple carving shows the king Indra trying to kill the serpent-dragon Vritra.

Monsters

CONTENTS

The world of monsters

The world's myths are full of creatures that are very different from those in real life. As they look strange and scary to us, we call them monsters.

Monsters come from a storyteller's imagination. Every time a story is told, the monster in the storyteller's mind grows bigger and scarier. It reaches a point when it's as big and as bad as it needs to be, and that's how it stays.

Myths about monsters have been told for thousands of years, by people all over the world. Many of these myths, such as those of the ancient Greeks from 2500 years ago, have become well known.

*The **werewolf** is a human that changes into a wolf during a full moon.*

Clay creatures

In the Middle Ages in Europe (about 800 years ago), Jewish folklore told of a human-like monster called a **golem** (meaning 'a clod of earth'). It was a servant that helped and protected its human master.

A golem was formed from clay, and came to life when it was put under a spell.

Who's who among monsters?

Flying Head
This is a giant head with wings for ears, wild hair, fiery eyes and rows of pointed fangs.

Griffin
A beast with the body of a lion and the head and wings of an eagle.

Great Serpent
A massive snake with a red head and scales of many colours.

Minotaur
This monster has the body of a man and the head of a bull.

Hydra
A giant ***serpent*** *with many heads and poisonous blood.*

Kraken
This enormous, horned sea monster dragged ships down to the seabed.

Harpy
A flying creature with the legs and wings of a vulture and the head and body of a woman.

Cerberus
A giant dog with three heads, each of which was covered in snakes.

Monsters with many heads

Some of the weirdest-looking monsters ever described are ones that have many heads.

⬆ *Cerberus, the three-headed dog.*

The ancient Greeks told stories about Cerberus, a fierce, three-headed dog. They also believed in the **Chimera**, which was a cross between a goat, a lion and a serpent, with heads growing out of its back. Then there was a race of giants called **Centimanes**, each of which had 50 heads, and a dragon called Ladon that had 100 heads!

Myth-makers in other parts of the world have also told tales about many-headed creatures. The **Vikings** of Scandinavia created myths about a six-headed giant called Thrudgelmir. He was said to be one of the first beings ever to have lived on Earth.

⬅ *The Hydra, from ancient Greek myth, was a deadly, multi-headed serpent.*

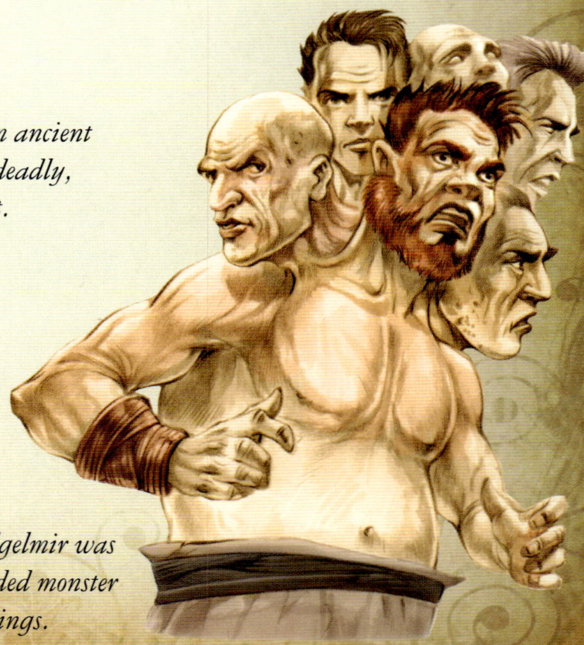

➡ *Thrudgelmir was a six-headed monster of the Vikings.*

Terrifying Typhon

Of all the monsters of ancient Greece, Typhon was the most terrifying. He had the body of a snake, huge dragon wings and fiery eyes. The god Zeus locked him away beneath the volcano Mount Etna, Sicily.

➡ This ancient Greek vase shows the god Zeus attacking Typhon, a huge, snake-like monster.

In the folktales of Scotland is a terrifying **ogre** called Red Etin. Not only did he have three heads, but he was also a **cannibal** that caught and ate people.

All these monsters were thought to be so dangerous that they could kill. Only the bravest of the brave would dare to fight them.

⬆ A Centimane was a scary, multi-headed giant from ancient Greece.

⬅ The three-headed ogre Red Etin of Scottish folktales.

Once upon a time:
How Heracles killed the Hydra

This myth comes from…

Long ago, people from ancient Greece talked of the greatest hero who had ever lived. His name was Heracles. He had been given 12 difficult tasks. One of them was to destroy the hideous Hydra.

The Hydra's heads grew back as fast as Heracles cut them off.

The Hydra was a giant serpent with many heads – some said five, some said 100. Its blood was poisonous, and so was its stinking breath. When the Hydra slithered from its swampy home, nothing was safe.

Heracles went to the Hydra's **lair**, as it was his duty to kill it. When the Hydra appeared, Heracles attacked its heads. But as soon as he cut off one head, two new ones grew in its place.

To make his task more difficult, a giant crab kept pinching his feet. Heracles called for help, and Iolaus (*say: ee-oh-lus*), his nephew, joined in the battle. The crab was first to die – Heracles smashed its shell with his foot.

Iolaus sealed the Hydra's necks with fire so its heads could not grow back.

Heracles, hero of the ancient Greeks, defeated the monstrous Hydra.

The Twelve Labours of Heracles

In a moment of madness, Heracles killed his own family. As punishment, he was told to work for King Eurystheus (say: yoo-rees-thee-oos). The king gave him 12 labours, or tasks, one of which was to kill the Hydra.

Then, Heracles sliced off the serpent's heads, and Iolaus touched the bleeding necks with a burning torch. The heat sealed the wounds so new heads could not grow. One by one the heads fell. When the last was cut off, the Hydra was dead. Heracles sliced open its body and took its poisoned blood to use on his arrow-tips.

Once upon a time:
How Heracles caught Cerberus

Cerberus was a fierce, three-headed dog that guarded the entrance to **Hades**, or the **underworld**. Heracles, hero of the Greeks, was ordered to capture it.

This was the last of the 12 labours, or tasks, that King Eurystheus had given him to do. The gates to Hades led to a cold, dark place below the Earth, where the souls of the dead were taken. Snake heads sprouted from Cerberus' back, and its tail was a serpent.

Cerberus welcomed souls to Hades, greeting them playfully. However, if any soul tried to leave, the dog ate it up.

➡ *Heracles was bitten by the snake that grew from the back of Cerberus.*

King Eurystheus told Heracles to capture Cerberus alive and bring him to the surface of the Earth. Hercules was forbidden to use weapons, so he had to rely on his own strength.

Heracles entered Hades, but there was no welcome from Cerberus. It pounced, and its tail-snake bit him. Heracles grabbed the monster and squeezed its throats until it nearly suffocated. Heracles bound it in chains and carried it into the world of the living.

King Eurystheus took one look at Cerberus and fled in terror.

Aconite looks pretty when it is in flower, but it is poisonous.

Poison plant

Spit from Cerberus' mouths that fell onto the ground was said to grow into aconite, a poisonous plant. It is known by many names, including monkshood and wolfsbane. It grows in northern parts of the world.

The sight of Cerberus was too much for King Eurystheus, who ran away in fear. Hercules unchained the monster, and it ran back to Hades. As for Heracles, his labours were over.

Serpents and sea monsters

⬆ *Sailors were terrified of monsters they believed could rise up from the sea and sink their ships.*

If ever there was a creature that, to a storyteller, would make the perfect monster, it was the snake. In the real world, many snakes are natural-born killers. They can squeeze or poison their victims to death.

What's more, snakes can grow to huge sizes, are found on land and in water, and move without making a sound. In myths, snakes became monstrous serpents. Some were big enough to wrap themselves around the whole world! They had poisonous bites, and some were given lots of heads. A common job for many serpents was to guard treasure or captured people – something they had in common with dragons.

Sinbad's monster

Sinbad the Sailor had many adventures in folktales of the Middle East. In one story, he thought he had come to an island in the middle of the ocean. He went ashore with his men, but when they lit a fire, the 'island' came to life and swam to the bottom of the sea. It wasn't an island, but the Zaratan – a giant sea turtle.

The Zaratan was so big that sailors mistook it for an island.

The sea was often the home of monsters – usually very big ones. Myths of the Middle East described a sea monster so big that sailors thought it was an island. They called it the Zaratan. To European sailors of the Middle Ages (around 800 years ago), there was a sea monster to fear above all others. It was called the **Kraken**, a monster that sank ships and drowned all on board.

*Giant **squid** were sea monsters that could attack and destroy entire ships.*

FROM SERPENT TO DRAGON

The idea of dragons may have come from serpents. As people began to imagine serpents with legs and wings, the dragon was invented.

Once upon a time:
The Great Serpent and the flood

The Great Serpent is a magical creature from the myths of the Chippewa people of North America.

⬆ *The Great Serpent dragged Nanabozho's cousin from their house.*

There was once a hero called Nanabozho (say: *nah-nah-boh-zhoh*), who lived with his cousin. One day, the Great Serpent entered their house, wrapped its coils around Nanabozho's cousin, and dragged him away.

Angrily, Nanabozho followed the serpent's tracks to a lake. Far below the water, he saw the monster in its lair, with the dead body of his cousin. Nanabozho called on the Sun to make the water so hot that the Great Serpent would have to come to the surface. Nanabozho hid behind a tree and waited.

This ancient drawing, made on a rock face, shows the Great Serpent.

Great Horned Serpent

Giant snakes are a part of many Native American myths. The Great Horned Serpent comes from stories of the Iroquois people. It is a gigantic rattlesnake that lives in a lake. The Iroquois believe that it protects them when they sail across the water.

Sure enough, the Great Serpent came out of the lake. Nanabozho fired an arrow into its heart, and the serpent fell back into the lake. As it thrashed about, giant waves crashed onto the shore. The land began to flood and covered the entire Earth.

After many days, the water grew calm. It was the sign Nanabozho had been waiting for. The Great Serpent was dead.

Nanabozho aimed his arrow at the Great Serpent's heart.

Once upon a time:
Arrow-Odd and the Sea-Reek

Sailors in northern seas around Scandinavia, Iceland and Greenland have told tales of a terrifying sea creature called the Kraken.

Long stories, known as **sagas**, were told by the Scandinavians during the Middle Ages. The saga of Arrow-Odd describes a sea monster that sounds very much like the Kraken, called the Sea-Reek.

Arrow-Odd and Vignir were the captains of two ships. One day, they saw two shapes that they thought were rocks rising from the sea. They sailed on, and came to an island they had never seen before. Some of the men went ashore for water. Suddenly, the island sank and the men were drowned.

← The monster slipped beneath the waves, and many men were drowned.

ANCIENT AMBER

Washed up on some northern shores are pieces of amber – a soft, smooth material that floats. Ancient sailors thought it was Kraken droppings! Today, we know that amber comes from ancient trees.

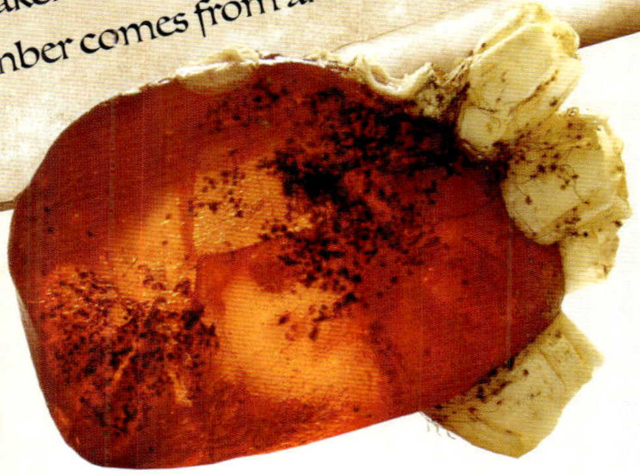

*Amber is **resin** from ancient trees, millions of years old.*

Arrow-Odd was deeply troubled. He asked Vignir, who was wiser than him, to explain what had happened. Vignir said they had found the monster Sea-Reek, the biggest monster in the ocean. It swallowed ships and whales, and could stay underwater for days. When it came to the surface, its body floated like an island. Its nostrils stood high above the water – these were the two rocks they thought they had seen. After hearing this, Arrow-Odd continued nervously on his journey.

Kraken close-up

The Kraken was said to measure up to 1.6 kilometres wide. When it swam to the seabed, it made a vast whirlpool. If ships were caught in the swirling waters, they were sucked down to join the monster.

The swirling water made by the Kraken was enough to drag a ship down to the seabed.

Monsters with wings

In myths, the land, air and water all have their own monsters. Walking, crawling and slithering monsters live on the land, and the sea is home to swimming monsters. Flying above all these are the monsters of the sky.

Fire-breathing dragons, giant birds and other creatures with wings – the sky is their domain. As long as they stay there, beyond the reach of humans, they are safe. However, when a winged monster comes too close to a human hero, the creature finds itself in trouble.

People have long believed in giant creatures with scaly skin and wings. The ancient Greeks told stories about Harpies – flying creatures with the bodies and wings of vultures and the heads and arms of old women.

⬆ *The **Roc** is said to look like a giant eagle.*

Elephant-carrying bird

The **Roc**, from Middle Eastern legend, was described as a bird of prey that looked like a giant eagle. It was so big it could carry an elephant in its claws!

Winged monsters were imagined in many different forms, from dragons to giant birds.

Not all flying monsters are so unreal. The Roc, from Middle Eastern myth, was simply a bird. However, it was much bigger than normal, and that is why it is known as a monster. And, just like other monsters, the Roc was scary because of what it did – it searched for prey to carry off and eat or feed to its young.

Vampires

Blood-sucking **vampires** are flying creatures that exist in the myths of many peoples. For example, the Choctaw tribe of North America describes a creature called the Skatene, and the Tamils of India have the Pey.

Vampires feed on the blood of humans.

Once upon a time:
How Jason defeated the Harpies

In the land of the ancient Greeks, Jason was given a difficult task. Pelias, a cruel king, had ordered him to fetch the Golden Fleece – a ram's skin made of gold.

As Jason went in search of the Golden Fleece, he arrived at the city of Salmydessus. A blind man called Phineus lived there, but he was in trouble. Two Harpies – flying creatures that were a cross between vultures and ugly old women – kept swooping down and snatching the food from Phineus' table. This left him forever hungry.

Jason asked Phineus how to find the Golden Fleece. Phineus promised to help on condition that Jason rid him of the Harpies. So Jason and his men, including Zetes and Calais who were able to fly, waited for the beasts to arrive.

➡ *The Harpies swooped to steal food from Phineus, but Zetes and Calais chased them away.*

When the Harpies came, the two men flew at them with swords, and they fled to a faraway island. Freed from the monsters, Phineus could eat in peace. In return, he helped Jason on his voyage to find the Golden Fleece.

⬆ *A Harpy painted on the side of an ancient Greek vase.*

Body-snatchers

The word 'harpy' means 'snatcher'. According to the ancient Greeks, a person lost at sea had been snatched by Harpies. Their human arms ended in the sharp talons of eagles, and once these had closed around a victim, there was no escape. They were surrounded by a terrible smell, and spoiled whatever they touched.

Once upon a time:
The griffins and their gold

Imagine a creature that is part-lion, part-eagle. This mighty beast is called a griffin – an animal with the body of a lion and the head and wings of a bird of prey.

The griffin was a greedy creature with fire-red eyes and large ears. It attacked anything that came near, as it was afraid they might be after the gold that it so jealously guarded.

The griffins fiercely guarded their gold from the thieving Arimaspians.

According to the ancient Greeks, griffins lived in Scythia, a region far to the north of Greece. They lived high up in the snowy mountains, and did so for good reason. The mountains were a source of gold, which the griffins dug up with their claws and beaks. The griffins loved the bright and shiny metal so much that they made their nests from it.

ALEXANDER AND THE GRIFFINS

Alexander the Great (lived 356 to 323 BC) was an important general of ancient Greece. It's said he chained eight griffins to a basket. He wanted them to fly him up to the heavens to meet the gods.

A race of one-eyed men called Arimaspians lived at the foot of the mountains. They climbed the mountaintops until they came upon the golden nests. As soon as they stole the gold, the griffins dug more gold and built new nests. The one-eyed thieves came for them again and again.

A hippogriff was part-horse and part-griffin. It was friendlier towards humans than griffins were.

Hippogriffs

A **hippogriff** is a beast with the rear of a horse and the front of a griffin. Unlike the wild griffins, hippogriffs can be tamed and used to carry human riders through the sky.

Humanoid monsters

Perhaps the scariest of all mythical monsters are the ones that look like humans. However, look closer and it's obvious they're not human at all. They are **humanoids** – creatures that have a mixture of human and non-human parts.

Humanoid monsters have existed in myths for thousands of years. For example, more than 3000 years ago, the people of ancient Iraq believed in a hideous giant called Humbaba. His face was a mass of coiled intestines, or guts.

Clay models of his face were hung inside houses. This was supposed to keep evil away. Perhaps evil was scared of Humbaba because he was so ugly!

⬆ Humbaba looked like a giant, hideous human.

➡ In Jewish legend, the golem was a human-like creature made of clay.

➡ *Mary Shelley's humanoid monster is known as 'Frankenstein's Monster'.*

⬆ *Medusa was a female monster whose gaze could turn people to stone.*

Humanoids also existed in the myths of the ancient Greeks. The **gorgons** were three terrifying sisters. One sister, called Medusa, had fangs in her mouth and her head was covered in snakes. If you looked into her eyes, you were turned instantly to stone.

Frankenstein's Monster

Humanoid monsters also appear in books. One of the best-known monsters was invented in 1818 by Mary Shelley. She described how a scientist, named Victor Frankenstein, made a monster from human body parts. His terrifying creation is known as 'Frankenstein's Monster'.

⬅ *The Minotaur, from ancient Greek myth, had the body of a man and the head of a bull.*

Myths tell of humanoid monsters that existed alongside humans. The stories mixed real-life places with made-up monsters. This caught people's attention, and they went away believing that these monsters really did exist.

Once upon a time: Theseus and the Minotaur

This myth comes from...

Long ago, on the Greek island of Crete, lived a flesh-eating monster called the Minotaur. It was part-man, part-bull.

The Minotaur was the prisoner of Minos, the king of Crete. He kept the beast in a great building called the **Labyrinth** (say: *la-ba-rinth*). Inside was a maze of passages from which there was no escape.

Every year, a ship sailed from Athens to Crete. On board were seven young men and seven young women, who were gifts from the people of Athens. Minos sent them into the Labyrinth, and one by one the Minotaur ate them.

Bull-leapers

The early people of Crete are known as Minoans, after Minos. Bulls were important to them. A wall painting at the palace of Knossos shows how they used to somersault over bulls by grabbing their horns.

➡ *This wall painting shows Minoans leaping over a bull.*

The real labyrinth

The palace at Knossos, Crete, was built about 1500 BC. When archaeologists uncovered it hundreds of years later, they discovered it had about 1000 rooms joined together. Its maze of rooms might have given Greek storytellers the idea for the Labyrinth.

↑ The ruins of the palace at Knossos, Crete, showing its maze of rooms.

One year, Theseus asked to be picked. He wanted to kill the Minotaur once and for all.

On Crete, Theseus met Ariadne, the daughter of King Minos, who gave him a ball of yarn. Theseus unwound the yarn as he walked inside the Labyrinth. There, he met the Minotaur, and struck it dead. Theseus followed the yarn back to the entrance, took Ariadne and the Athenians with him and set sail for home.

↓ Inside the Labyrinth, Theseus came face-to-face with the Minotaur.

Once upon a time:
The old woman and the Flying Head

This myth comes from...

A very odd humanoid monster exists in the folk tales of the Iroquois Native American people. It is known as the Flying Head.

That's all it is – a huge, wrinkled head with black wings for ears, fiery eyes, wild hair and sharp teeth.

The Flying Head flies at night. It moans as it rushes towards sleeping humans, especially women and children. It beats its wings against their homes and then, after a few days, someone in the house dies. This is because the Flying Head is the messenger of death.

The Flying Head was hungry for the old woman's acorns.

The Iroquois lived in fear of the Flying Head. One night, it visited the lodge of an old woman. She had lived a long life, and wisdom was her strength. She knew the monster would come for her, and she prepared herself for it. A fire was always burning in her cabin, and on it the old woman kept a pile of red-hot stones. As she sat by her fire, she roasted acorns for her evening meal.

TELLING TALES

Like all myths, the tale of the old woman and the Flying Head began as a spoken story. The people who heard it told it to their children, who did the same to their children. At some point, the story was written down and printed in a book, and so it was saved for future families to read.

Native American children listen to a storyteller's tale. In time they will pass it on to their children.

The Flying Head watched the old woman, and when it saw her eat the acorns, it wanted some, too. It flew into the room, but instead of gobbling up the acorns, its mouth closed around the red-hot stones. Nothing could ever fall out of its mouth, and as the fire stones began to burn it, the creature spun around in agony until it died.

Giants

CONTENTS

The world of giants

⬆ *In the Bible story, David (right) challenges the mighty Goliath in battle.*

The myths and legends of the world are full of stories about giants and giantesses. These are massive creatures with great strength, but their huge size is not matched by big brains.

Giants tend to be rather slow-witted and can be easily fooled. This is their greatest weakness. They might be able to throw huge rocks and shake the ground with their footsteps, but a human will always outsmart a giant.

There have been many **races** of giants, and most of them lived when the world was very young. As time passed, the giants fought and lost battles. The few that survived were thrown into prisons, or went into hiding.

Big and bigger

There is an ancient Jewish story about a very tall man called Goliath. He was nearly 3 metres tall – much taller than everyone else! The word 'goliath' is now used to describe big things, from giant beetles to huge trucks.

Who's who among the giants?

Trolls

Trolls are gruesome creatures that guard treasure in underground places.

Jotun

These are giants of the air, frost, mountains and water.

Gigantes (Greek giants)

Gigantes are terrible, violent creatures with snakes' bodies for legs.

Ogres

Ogres are similar to trolls, but are scarier and much more beastlike.

Centimanes

Three hideous brothers, each with 50 heads and 100 arms.

Cyclopes

These are savage monsters, each with a single eye in its forehead.

Fomorians

These are monsters with vile bodies. Each one has a leg, an arm, an eye and three rows of teeth.

Giants of ancient Greece

⬆ A ***Hundred-Hander***, *a Gigante, and a Cyclops – three giants of ancient Greece.*

The ancient Greeks believed in many different kinds of giants, and told wonderful stories about them. The greatest of these monstrous creatures were known as the Gigantes.

They were strong and dangerous, and had long, untidy hair. Instead of legs, they slithered about on the bodies of huge snakes. Stories explained that the Gigantes were the children of Gaia, the Earth goddess. Gaia was angry because her other children had been taken from her by new gods that lived on Mount Olympus.

One-eyed giants

In the myths of ancient Greece, the Cyclopes were three ugly giants. Each Cyclops had a single eye in the middle of its forehead. Their name means 'round-eyed'. The Cyclopes lived beneath the volcano, Mount Etna, on the island of Sicily in southern Italy.

In revenge, she created the Gigantes. As soon as they were created, the Gigantes began to help their mother. She ordered them to destroy the **Olympian** gods, and there was a terrible war.

HUNDRED-HANDED GIANTS

The Centimanes were three giants with 50 heads and 100 hands. Their name means 'hundred-handed'. They were the brothers of the Cyclopes, and they guarded prisoners of the gods.

Mount Olympus is said to be home to the gods of ancient Greece.

The Giants tossed boulders and burning trees at the gods, but their efforts came to nothing. Despite their great strength, they had a serious weakness.

They could be killed if a human fought with the gods – and that's what happened. A human called Heracles (say: *heh-ra-cleez*) helped the gods, and, one by one, the Gigantes were defeated.

Heracles and the gods of ancient Greece destroyed the terrible Gigantes using huge rocks, ***thunderbolts*** *and arrows.*

Once upon a time:
How Odysseus tricked the Cyclops

This myth comes from…

Long ago, there was a giant called Polyphemus (say: pol-ee-feem-oos). He was a Cyclops – a fierce, one-eyed monster.

One day, Odysseus (*say: o-dee-see-oos*), who was a Greek hero, visited an island and came to Polyphemus' cave. He went inside and found a flock of sheep. When the giant saw Odysseus, he blocked the cave entrance with a boulder. Odysseus was trapped inside, and feared for his life.

It's Nobody!

Odysseus told Polyphemus that his name was 'Nobody'. When Polyphemus was blinded, he cried out in pain. Other Cyclopes asked who was attacking him, and because Polyphemus said it was 'Nobody', the giants went away.

The blinded Polyphemus searched his cave for Odysseus.

That night, as Polyphemus slept, Odysseus stabbed him in the eye and made him blind. Then, he hid from Polyphemus by clinging onto the belly of a sheep. The blinded Polyphemus stumbled and felt around the cave for Odysseus.

Odysseus escaped to safety by clinging to the belly of a sheep.

As long as the giant's fingers touched only the soft, woolly back of the sheep, Odysseus knew he was safe. After a while, Polyphemus moved the boulder away from the cave entrance. His flock ran from the cave to their pasture, and that is how the cunning Odysseus escaped to safety.

Built by giants

The ancient Greeks thought the walls of some of their oldest cities had been built by giants. They believed that only giants had the strength to move such massive stones. Ancient walls such as this are called **Cyclopean walls.**

The ancient city of Tiryns, Greece, is surrounded by a wall of giant blocks of stone.

Once upon a time:
The war against the Gigantes

This myth comes from…

Of all the heroes of ancient Greece, there was none greater than Heracles. A war was looming between the gods of Mount Olympus and the Gigantes.

The gods could not defeat the Gigantes without help from a human, and as Heracles had more courage than any other **mortal**, they chose him.

The Gigantes lived among the volcanoes of a place called the **Burning Lands**. This is where the greatest battle of the war was fought. The strongest of all the Gigantes were the brothers Alcyoneus (say: *al-ky-on-ee-oos*) and Porphyrion (say: *por-fy-ree-on*).

The god Zeus struck down Porphyrion with a thunderbolt.

As they moved towards the gods, the Gigantes hurled massive rocks at them. When Alcyoneus was within range, Heracles shot him with a poisoned arrow. The monster came crashing down. He was hurt, but as long as he stayed within the Burning Lands, he could not die. Heracles dragged him away, and once they were beyond the Burning Lands, Alcyoneus was destroyed.

⬆ Brought down by a thunderbolt from Zeus, Porphyrion lay on the ground where the poisoned arrows of Heracles killed him

Next came Porphyrion. He was in a fearful rage, but the great god Zeus struck him down with a thunderbolt thrown from the heavens. Then the poisoned arrows of Heracles finished him off.

⬇ Heracles killed the Hydra monster to use its poisonous blood on his arrow-tips.

Poisoned arrows

The poison that Heracles used against the Gigantes came from the Hydra. This was a monster in the shape of a giant serpent with many heads. Heracles killed the Hydra and cut open its body. He then took its poisonous blood to use as venom on his arrow-tips.

Odious ogres, hideous hags

Giants appear in many fairy tales from Europe, where the men are called ogres and the women are called **hags**. In many cases they are simply known as 'beasts', and for good reason.

Ogres and hags look like humans, but are much bigger in size. They are incredibly strong, but they are also stupid, slow-moving and very ugly. The worst thing about them is their taste for human flesh, and that's what makes them so very scary.

⬆ *Artists have always pictured a hag, or crone, as a wrinkled old woman.*

⬅ *Shrek the ogre gets his name from the German word* schreck, *meaning 'terror'.*

An ogre is born

Ogres are still being invented today. In 2001, the lead role in the movie 'Shrek' was an ogre. But Shrek the ogre is a friendly character, very different from the ogres in traditional stories.

⬆ *In the fairy tale 'Jack and the Beanstalk', Jack stole a magic harp from the giant.*

Hags can live for a very long time, which is why they are called Old Hags or Undying Hags. One hag called Black Annis (or Black Agnes) is said to live in a cave in the Dane Hills, near Leicester, England. She has a blue face, yellow teeth and long, iron claws. At dusk, she leaves her cave and hunts humans who have stayed out too late on the hills. Once in her grip, a poor soul is gobbled up.

From bones to bread

The giant in the well-known fairy tale 'Jack and the Beanstalk' is a human-gobbling ogre. He promises to turn poor Jack's bones into powder, which he'll use to make his bread:

"Fee! Fie! Foe! Fum!
I smell the blood of an Englishman.
Be he alive, or be he dead,
I'll grind his bones to make my bread."

Anyone for a hag's dish?

Haggis is a traditional food from Scotland, made with meat and spices. No one knows how haggis got its name. One idea is that it means 'hag's dish' – a mix of body parts eaten by bloodthirsty hags!

Once upon a time:
Baba Yaga and Vasilisa the Brave

There was once a lovely young girl called Vasilisa, whose evil stepmother was always cruel to her.

One day, the candle in Vasilisa's house went out, and her stepmother told her to bring fire from Baba Yaga, the woman who lived in the woods. Baba Yaga was a horrible old hag, and Vasilisa was frightened of her.

⬆ *Baba Yaga was a crooked old hag who flew around the woods in a grinding bowl.*

Now, before Vasilisa's real mother died, she gave her a magic wooden doll. As Vasilisa made her way to Baba Yaga's house, the doll spoke and said she would not let any harm come to her. Vasilisa came to a clearing in the woods, and there was the hag's strange-looking house. It was whirling around on hens' legs! The old hag took Vasilisa inside, and from then on she was a prisoner.

Each day, Baba Yaga gave her tasks, saying that if they weren't done, she would eat the girl for tea. When the old hag wasn't looking, Vasilisa's doll helped her. When asked how she had done the work, Vasilisa said, "By my mother's love." Baba Yaga hated the mention of 'love', and told Vasilisa to take the fire she had come for and go home.

Vasilisa left. The fire she took glowed from inside a skull. When her wicked stepmother saw it, she burst into flames! From then on, Vasilisa was free to live as she wished.

THE BONY-LEGGED ONE

Baba Yaga is also known as the Bony-Legged One. She is described as a flesh-eating hag with fangs and a hooked nose. Her gaze can turn people to stone. She flies around in a mortar (a bowl used for grinding food).

One look at Baba Yaga's flame and Vasilisa's evil stepmother burst into flames.

Giants of northern lands

The lands of Scandinavia and northern Europe are rich in stories about giants. Long ago, this region was the home of the **Vikings**, who told amazing tales of the Jotun (say: yo-tun), or giants.

Viking stories say the Jotun existed at the very beginning of time, and were the first living things on Earth. The Jotun made the world a very dangerous place to live.

A Frost Giant – one of the mighty Jotun.

*The snowy mountains of **Jotunheim**, or Giantland, are said to be home to the Jotun.*

Giantland

In Norway there is a region known as Jotunheim (say: yo-tun-hime), meaning 'Giantland'. This is where the Jotun are said to live, among the cold, snow-covered mountains.

The Jotun looked like humans, but with massive bodies. They could be very ugly. Some, such as Thrivaldi ("Thrice Mighty") had many heads – he had nine in total. They lived in mountain caves in icy places. Sometimes the Jotun were helpful to humans, but they also had bad tempers.

The Jotun are divided into four groups – Air Giants, such as Kari (meaning 'Tempest'), Frost Giants, such as Thrym ('Frost'), Water Giants, such as Gymir ('Sea'), and Mountain Giants, such as Senjeman from the island of Senjen.

Terrible trolls

Scandinavia is also home to creatures called trolls. Some are as big as giants, others are tiny. They are all ugly and hairy with hunched backs. They live underground, where they guard valuable treasures. If the Sun shines on them, they are turned to stone.

← Trolls live in underground places, where they guard great treasures.

Once upon a time:
Why Thrym took the magic hammer

Thor was the mightiest of the Viking gods. He defended both gods and humans against the Jotun, or giants. But this was only possible as long as his magic hammer, Mjöllnir (say: me-yoll-near), was with him.

The Jotun knew that the secret of Thor's power lay in his great hammer, so they plotted to steal it. Thrym, a Frost Giant, took Mjöllnir, and he buried it in the land of the giants.

➨ *The giant Thrym was easily fooled by Thor's clever plan.*

LUCKY CHARM

Thor's Hammer, or Mjöllnir, was made by **dwarfs** in their underground workshops. Viking men and women often carried tiny copies of Mjöllnir as lucky charms to keep them safe from harm.

➡ *A Viking lucky charm, made in the shape of Thor's Hammer.*

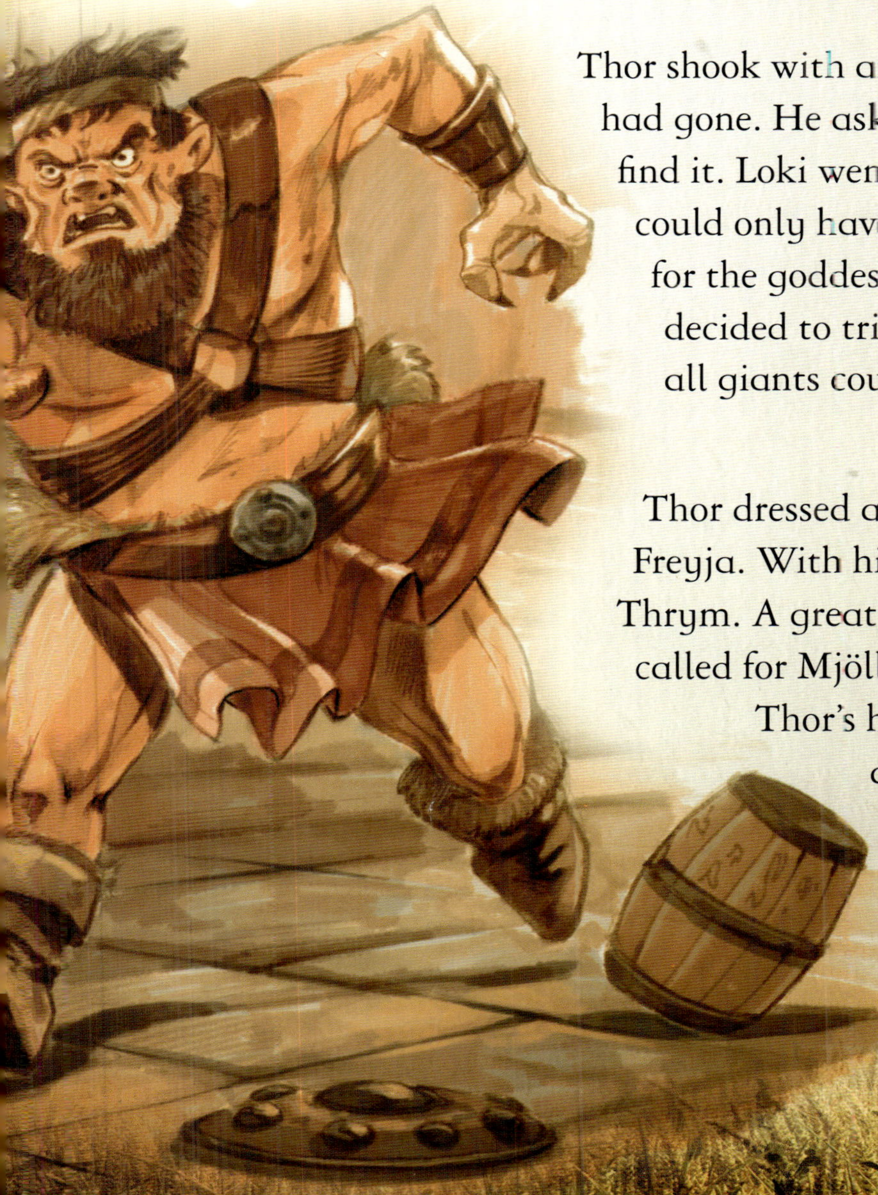

Thor shook with anger to find that Mjöllnir had gone. He asked the god Loki to help him find it. Loki went to Thrym, who said they could only have the hammer in exchange for the goddess Freyja (say: *fray-a*). Thor decided to trick Thrym, for he knew that all giants could be easily fooled.

Thor dressed as a bride and pretended to be Freyja. With his face behind a veil, he went to Thrym. A great wedding feast was set. Thrym called for Mjöllnir, and when it was placed in Thor's hand he turned it on the giant and struck him dead. From then on, Mjöllnir was known as Thor'sHammer, and the two were never parted again.

Once upon a time:
The trolls in Hedal Woods

This myth comes from...

Two brothers were out walking in Hedal Woods, in Norway. It grew late, and darkness fell quickly. The boys realized they were trapped among the trees.

They gathered branches and made a shelter for the night. They had barely closed their eyes when they heard a snuffling and a scuffling from outside. The noises grew louder and the ground began to shake. The boys knew that the three trolls of Hedal Woods were upon them.

The older brother chased after the trolls with a knife.

The trolls shared one eye between them. Each troll had a hole in its forehead, and whoever placed the eye in its socket was the only one that could see. The seeing troll led the way, and the blind trolls followed.

The younger brother ran, and the trolls chased him. The older brother came after the trolls and chopped the ankle of the slowest one. It screamed, and this gave the seeing troll such a fright that it dropped the eye.

The trolls pleaded with the boys to give back their precious eye.

Mistletoe is a poisonous plant that grows on and lives off a tree or a shrub.

The boys picked up the trolls' eye, and all three trolls let out a roar as loud as thunder. The brothers let them roar, for they knew that as long as the trolls could not see, they were safe.

The trolls pleaded with the brothers, and agreed to give them gold and silver in return for their eye. They also promised never to harm anyone else that wandered into Hedal Woods.

Keeping trolls away

Trolls are said to steal women, children, animals and belongings. Humans can protect themselves from the trolls by placing **mistletoe** around their house.

Giants of Britain and Ireland

It was once believed that all of Britain and Ireland, in the UK, was home to giants.

In Britain there were three brothers – Albion, Gog, and Magog – who, so ancient stories say, were defeated by an invading army of humans. In Ireland, a race of giants known as the Fomorians were said to have first lived on the island.

The Fomorians were hideous creatures with human bodies, the heads of goats, and only one eye, one arm and one leg each. All of Ireland was theirs, but in time they were defeated in battle and they disappeared.

The Fomorians were gruesome giants from Ireland.

The Long Man of Wilmington is a giant figure cut into the white chalk of a hill.

Chalk giant

Carved into a hill near the village of Wilmington, England, is a giant known as the Long Man of Wilmington. He is 69 metres tall! A story says that an enemy giant knocked him over, and the outline of his body was cut into the hill where he fell.

The giant Gog is paraded through the streets of London for the Lord Mayor's Show.

Giants on parade

The City of London is said to be guarded by the giants Gog and Magog. Since the 1500s, giant-sized figures of them have been paraded each year at the Lord Mayor's Show.

As for Albion, Gog and Magog, the memory of them did not die with them. For hundreds of years, Britain was known as 'Albion'. Statues of Gog and Magog were put up outside the Guildhall, the City of London's town hall.

STONE CIRCLE

Stonehenge is an ancient **stone circle** in Wiltshire, England. It was once known as the Giants' Dance. Legend says it was built by giants, who placed it on a mountain in Ireland, and then later it was brought to England.

Some say the ancient stone circle of Stonehenge, England, was built by giants.

Once upon a time:
How Finn McCool fooled Fingal

This myth comes from...

Finn McCool was a giant who came from Ireland. He lived on a headland that poked out into the sea, in the direction of Scotland.

Finn McCool hurled boulders across the sea to make a pathway for him to walk on.

One day, a Scottish giant called Fingal spied Finn McCool from across the water. Fingal called Finn McCool names and this made the Irish giant very angry.

Finn McCool took up a great clump of soil and hurled it at Fingal. It missed, and splashed into the sea. Fingal laughed, and tossed back a massive rock.

The Giant's Causeway

The Giant's Causeway is an area of Northern Ireland that is made up of amazing rock formations. These were caused millions of years ago by volcanic eruptions.

➡ *The Giant's Causeway stretches out to sea as far as the Scottish island of Staffa. In the story of Finn McCool, this is the pathway he made.*

This only made Finn McCool angrier, and for the next week he hurled rock after rock into the sea, until he had made a great pathway that joined Ireland to Scotland. Now the giants could fight each other face to face.

⬆ *Fingal's Cave, on the island of Staffa, Scotland.*

Fingal's Cave

The Scottish end of the Giant's Causeway is on the island of Staffa. A cave on the island is called Fingal's Cave, which is where Fingal is said to be in hiding.

But, by now, Finn McCool was too tired to go to Fingal. So he came up with a plan. He dressed as a baby and lay down in a cot. When Fingal stormed across to Finn McCool's house, he saw what he thought was a baby. If the baby is as big as a giant, he thought, how much bigger Finn McCool must be! And with this, Fingal fled back to Scotland and hid inside a cave.

Giants of America

Giants have a special place in the traditional stories of the Native Americans of Canada and the USA. There are tales of giants that are kind to humans, and others that are to be feared, such as the **Sasquatch** and the Coeur d'Alene Tree Men.

Stories of giants known as Tree Men come from the Coeur d'Alene people. This tribe's homeland is now made up of Idaho, eastern Washingtonand western Montana. Taller than teepees, the Tree Men were hairy and had a bad smell. They could change into trees or bushes, and they ate fish, which they stole from people's traps.

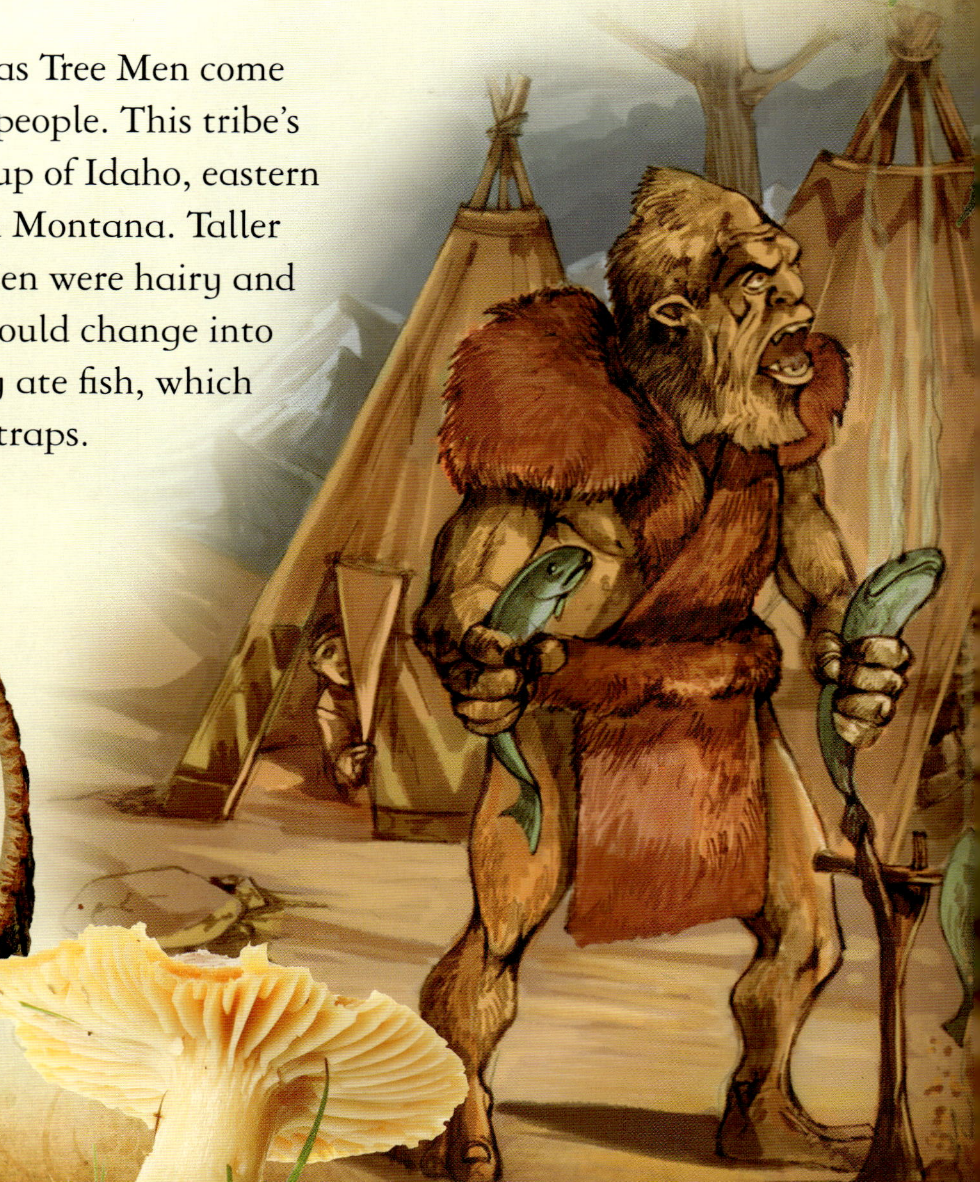

The Coeur d'Alene people lived in fear of the Tree Men.

Helpful giant

The Iroquois people of northeastern USA tell tales of a helpful giant called Split-Face. His body is red on one side and black on the other. He protects people from evil.

CAUGHT ON FILM

In 1967, Roger Patterson and Robert Gimlin said they had filmed a **Bigfoot** in California. To this day, no one is sure if the film really does show a giant, hairy animal or if it's just a man dressed up as Bigfoot.

⬆ *This photograph may show Bigfoot – but it could be a fake.*

The native peoples of western Canada and northwest USA tell stories of a giant creature that walks like a man and is covered in long, shaggy hair. Some stories say it stands 4.5 metres tall. It has many names, but Sasquatch, meaning 'wild man', is the one that now joins them all together. A more popular name for it is Bigfoot.

Once upon a time:
Paul Bunyan, the giant lumberjack

There was once a baby boy named Paul Bunyan. He was so big he wore his father's clothes, and his cry was so loud that frogs jumped from their ponds.

On his first birthday, Paul's father gave him a blue ox named Babe. As Paul grew, so did Babe, and soon everyone knew about the giant boy and his giant ox.

When Paul became a man, he took a job as a **lumberjack**. He worked all day with seven big, strong axemen, cutting down trees with one swing of his axe.

➡ *Paul Bunyan and his axemen at work.*

One year, it was so cold it felt as if there were two winters. Paul worked right through. When he spoke, his words froze in mid-air. When the air thawed out in the spring, his chattering voice was heard for weeks.

⬆ *Paul Bunyan worked hard through the long, cold winter.*

All-American hero

The tales of Paul Bunyan were first told in the late 1800s. They proved so popular that today he is something of an all-American hero. A few towns have put up giant statues in his honour.

He used giant mosquitoes to drill holes in wood, and giant worker ants to haul logs from the forest. No task was ever too big for Paul Bunyan, and no deed was too difficult. If help was needed, Paul Bunyan, the giant lumberjack, would save the day.

The Grand Canyon

The Grand Canyon is a huge, deep, rocky valley in Arizona, USA. It was said that Paul Bunyan created the Grand Canyon when he dragged his axe across the ground.

⬅ *The Grand Canyon is 365 kilometres long, 29 kilometres wide and about 1.5 kilometres deep.*

GLOSSARY

Baptize To give a child its name during a special Christian ceremony known as a baptism.

Beltane An ancient festival held on 1 May to mark the start of summer.

Bigfoot A giant creature from the myths of western Canada and northwest USA. It is said to walk like a man and look like a huge, hairy animal. It is also known as a Sasquatch.

Burial mound An ancient mound of soil placed over the burial place (grave) of a dead person.

Burning Lands A place where the Gigantes lived, among the burning hot volcanoes.

Cannibal A person who eats human flesh, or an animal that eats animals of its own kind.

Centimanes Giants from the myths of ancient Greece with 50 heads and 100 arms. Also known as Hundred-Handers.

Changeling A fairy baby swapped, or changed, for a human baby.

Chimera A monster from the myths of ancient Greece that was a cross between a goat, a lion and a serpent.

Clan A group of fairies that all live together.

Coral A hard red, pink or white substance formed from the skeletons of tiny sea creatures. They grow beneath the sea, and are often found in groups that form a reef.

Cursed When a curse has been put on a person, a place or an object, so that something bad or harmful happens.

Cyclopean An adjective used to describe a building or a wall that is so big it could have been built by giants.

Dragonship A type of warship used by the Vikings, with a carved image of a dragon at the prow (front).

Dragon-slayer A person who slays (kills) a dragon.

Dragon-stone A type of red stone thought to be formed from dragon's blood that has set hard.

Drought A long period of time without any rainfall.

Dwarfs Hard-working fairies that live underground. Their special gift is to turn jewels and other riches into beautiful objects.

Elf arrows The name given to arrow heads made from pieces of flint. They were made thousands of years ago, but before that was known, it was thought they were made by elves.

Fairy godmother A kind fairy who helps and protects a human as if the person was their own child.

Famine A serious shortage of food that causes terrible hunger and even starvation.

Fay Another word for fairy.

Golem A humanoid monster from Jewish myths that was formed from clay. It was a servant that helped and protected its human masters.

Gorgon A humanoid monster from the myths of ancient Greece whose head was covered in snakes. If a person looked into its eyes, they were turned to stone.

Hades In the myths of ancient Greece, Hades is the Land of the Dead – the place below the Earth where the souls of the dead are taken.

Hag An ugly old female giant from the myths of Europe, also known as an ogress. A male is called an ogre. Hags are stupid creatures that are easily fooled by humans.

Haggis A traditional food from Scotland. It is usually made from the chopped-up lungs, heart and liver of a sheep, mixed with onion, oatmeal, spices, and salt.

Hippocamp In the myths of ancient Greece, a sea creature that was part-horse, part-fish.

Hippogriff A beast with the rear of a horse and the front of a griffin, from the myths of ancient Greece.

House fairy A fairy that lives in a human's house, where it usually does helpful work.

Humanoid A monster that is similar to a human.

Hundred-Handers Another name for the Centimanes – giants from the myths of ancient Greece that each had 50 heads and 100 arms.

Iron A hard metal that is used to make steel.

Jade A hard, green stone that can be carved to make jewellery and ornaments.

Jotunheim A region in Norway where the Jotun, or giants, were said to live at the beginning of the world. The name means Giantland.

Kraken A gigantic sea monster from the myths of Northern Europe.

Labyrinth A confusing maze of rooms and passages in the myths of ancient Greece. At the centre of the Labyrinth lived the Minotaur.

Lair The place where an animal, often a dangerous one, lives.

Longship A narrow warship used to transport Viking soldiers.

Lumberjack Someone who cuts down trees for their job.

Middle Ages A period of time in European history that starts around AD 450 and ends around AD 1500.

Milk tooth A tooth in the first set of a baby's teeth.

Mistletoe A plant with white berries that grows on trees. It is a parasite – it lives off the tree it grows on, and can cause it harm.

Mortal An ordinary human being who doesn't have any superhuman or magical powers.

Nereids In the myths of ancient Greece, the Nereids were a group of 50 nature fairies.

Ogre A male giant from the myths of Europe. A female is an ogress or a hag. Ogres and ogresses are stupid creatures that are easily fooled by humans. They are very strong, and some are said to be cannibals.

Olympian An adjective used to describe the gods of ancient Greece that lived on a mountain called Mount Olympus.

Patron saint A saint who is seen as the special protector of a country or place.

Pendragon A name given to warriors from Wales, UK, in the Middle Ages. It means 'dragon head'.

Phoenix A mythical bird that is said to live for hundreds of years and then die in a fire. It then rises up from the ashes as a young bird, ready to live again.

Race The family to which a particular type of giant belongs.

Resin A see-through substance that comes from the sap of trees.

Roc A giant bird of prey in the myths of the Middle East.

Saga A long story told by the Vikings about their gods, monsters, kings, and history.

Saint A man or woman who leads a very holy life. Christians, as well as members of some other religions, worship saints.

Samhain An ancient festival held on 31 October to mark the start of winter.

Sasquatch Also known as Bigfoot, this hairy giant is said to roam the wild parts of Canada and northwest USA. Its name means 'wild man'.

Serpent A very large snake. In stories and folktales, huge, terrifying snakes are often called serpents.

Shape-shifter A fairy that can change shape from one thing to another.

Shrine A religious place where people to go to worship a particular god or person.

Solar eclipse An event that happens when the Moon passes between the Sun and the Earth. The Sun is blocked out, making it appear dark, even in the middle of the day.

Solitary fairies Shy, secretive fairies that live alone, and always stay close to their homes.

Sprite A general word used to describe any type of fairy.

Squid A sea animal, like an octopus, with eight arms and two tentacles.

Standard A type of flag carried into battle, or flown from a building.

Stone circle Large stones arranged so that they stand upright in a circle, made by the people of ancient Europe, particularly Britain and Ireland. The most famous stone circle in Britain is Stonehenge.

Thunderbolt A lightning flash and a clap of thunder that happens together. In ancient Greece, Zeus, the king of the gods, had the power to throw thunderbolts down to Earth.

Toad-stone A stone that people thought lay inside toads. The stone was worn as a lucky charm, as people believed it would protect them from harm.

Tooth fairy A fairy that leaves a gift, such as money, under a child's pillow when one of the child's milk teeth falls out.

Trooping fairies Fairies that live in clans, or groups, and like to march, or troop, in processions.

Underworld An underground place where the spirits of the dead live.

Vampire A blood-sucking monster, usually pictured as a bat with fangs.

Vikings A group of people that came from Scandinavia, in the north of Europe. The Viking Age began about 1200 years ago and lasted for 300 years.

Werewolf A monster from myths around the world that is said to be able to change from a wolf into a human being, and back again.

Will-o'-the-wisp A ball of fire, seen at night, that moves close to the ground over moors and heaths.

INDEX